Fox's Cave

retold by Pam Holden
illustrated by Samer Hatam

One morning a hungry fox was waiting
outside his cave.
He saw a fat duck walking by.
"Good morning, Duck," said Fox.
"You look hungry today.
Come into my cave for breakfast."

2

"Thank you," said Duck.
"I'm very hungry this morning."
She went inside the cave with Fox.

Soon Fox was waiting outside again.
A fat hen came walking along.
"Good morning, Hen," called Fox.
"Would you like to come into my cave
for some breakfast?"

"Yes, I would like that," said Hen.
"I want something to eat."
She walked into Fox's cave.

Before long, a fat goose walked by.
"Good morning, Goose," said Fox.
"You look hungry this morning.
Come into my cave for breakfast."

"Yes, I'm ready for some breakfast,"
said Goose.
She followed Fox into his cave.

Later Fox was waiting outside again.
He saw a big bird hopping along.
"Good afternoon, Bird," called Fox.
"Would you like to come into my
cave for some lunch?"

"Yes, please," said Bird.
"I'm very hungry this afternoon."
She hopped into Fox's cave.

Before long, a fat rooster came by.
"Good afternoon, Rooster," said Fox.
"You could come into my cave for
some lunch."

"Thanks. I would like some lunch,"
said Rooster.
He followed Fox into the cave.

Later a fat rabbit came hopping along.
"Hello, Rabbit," said Fox.
"You look very hungry today.
Come into my cave for dinner."

"Thank you," said Rabbit.
"I'm ready for some dinner."
He hopped inside the cave with Fox.

Before long, Monkey came running by.
"Hello, Monkey," called Fox.
"Are you looking for something to eat?
Come into my cave for dinner."

14

"No, thanks," said Monkey. "Not me!
I don't want to go inside your cave.
I saw Hen and Goose and Duck go in.
Rabbit and Rooster and Bird all
went inside, too."

Monkey didn't stop running.
He called to Fox, "Where are they now?
Why has nobody come back out of your
cave, Fox?"